Franklin
GOES TO SCHOOL

Franklin is a trade mark of Kids Can Press Ltd.

No part of this publication may be reproduced in whole or in
part, or stored in a retrieval system, or transmitted in any form,
or by any means, electronic, mechanical, photocopying, record-
ing, or otherwise, without written permission of the publisher.
For information regarding permission, write to Kids Can Press
Ltd., 29 Birch Avenue, Toronto, Ontario, Canada M4V 1E2.

ISBN 0-590-25467-7

Text copyright © 1995 by P.B. Creations Inc.
Illustrations copyright © 1995 by Brenda Clark Illustrator Inc.
Interior illustrations prepared with the assistance of Dimitrije
Kostic.

All rights reserved. Published by Scholastic Inc., 555 Broadway,
New York, NY 10012, by arrangement with Kids Can Press Ltd.
SCHOLASTIC and associated logos are trademarks and/or
registered trademarks of Scholastic Inc.

24 23 22 21 20   0 1 2 3/0

Printed in the U.S.A.   23

First Scholastic printing, September 1995

Franklin
GOES TO SCHOOL
Paulette Bourgeois • Brenda Clark

SCHOLASTIC INC.
New York Toronto London Auckland Sydney

FRANKLIN could count by twos and tie his shoes. He could zip zippers and button buttons. But Franklin was worried about starting school. And that was a problem because Franklin was going to school for the very first time.

Franklin woke up with the sun. "It's my first day of school!" he told Goldie, his fish.

Franklin packed his new pencil case with a ruler, a pencil, an eraser, and twelve colored pencils that he had sharpened himself.

Then he woke his parents.

"Hurry," he said to his parents. "I cannot be late for school."

Franklin's mother looked at the clock. "Even the teacher is not awake," she laughed. "It is too early."

"You must be very excited," said Franklin's father.

Franklin nodded.

It was so early that there was time to make a big breakfast.

"You'll need a full tummy to work at school," said Franklin's father.

Franklin was not hungry. "I already have a full tummy," he said. "It feels like it is full of jumping frogs."

Franklin's mother gave him a hug. "I felt that way on my first day of school. But the funny feeling went away."

Franklin ate a little. He double-checked his book bag. Finally, it was time to go to school.

Halfway to the bus stop, Franklin clutched his tummy.

"I don't want to go," he said.

Franklin's father gave him a hug. "That's how I felt when I started school," he said. "Look. All your friends are waiting for the bus."

There was a big crowd at the bus stop. There were brothers and sisters and mothers and fathers.

Beaver was carrying her favorite book. "I can read it," she said.

"All of it?" asked Bear.

"Yes," she answered proudly.

Franklin rubbed his tummy.

Rabbit pulled out a brand-new notebook. "My big sister showed me how to write my numbers," he said.

"All of them?" asked Fox.

"Most of them," boasted Rabbit.

Franklin looked at his mother. "I want to go home," he said.

"We will be here after school to hear about all the things you did today," she said.

When the bus arrived, Rabbit grabbed his sister's hand and climbed aboard. Bear stood on the steps and waved good-bye again and again. Franklin hugged his mother, then his father. He kept hugging even after his friends had found seats.

As the bus pulled away, Franklin looked out the window. He didn't know if he was ready for school.

"Do you think the teacher will yell?" wondered Rabbit, who jumped at loud noises.

"Do you think there's a bathroom at school?" asked Beaver, fidgeting in her seat.

"I hope somebody has an extra snack," said Bear, who had already eaten his.

Franklin did not say anything. The bus ride seemed very, very long.

When they arrived, their teacher was waiting.

Mr. Owl said hello in a gentle voice. He showed them where to hang their coats and where to sit. He showed them where to find the bathroom and offered everyone a piece of fruit.

Then, Beaver and Bear went to the reading and writing center. Rabbit went to the play kitchen. But Franklin stayed in his seat.

"What would you like to do today, Franklin?" asked Mr. Owl.

"I don't know," said Franklin, rubbing his tummy. "I cannot write all the numbers like Rabbit can. I cannot read like Beaver can."

"Rabbit and Beaver will learn new things at school, and so will you."

Franklin started to doodle.

"I can see that you are a very good artist," said the teacher.

Franklin sat up taller. "I know all my colors, too," he said.

"What color is this?" asked Mr. Owl, holding up a colored pencil.

"It's a special blue," said Franklin. "It is turquoise."

"Now you have taught *me* something," said Mr. Owl. "Is there something special *you* would like to learn?"

There were so many things Franklin wanted to learn that he had trouble deciding.

Finally, he asked Mr. Owl to help him read his favorite book.

Franklin made a building of blocks.

He sorted the money in the classroom store and painted four pictures. One for the teacher, one for himself, and two for his parents.

It was a wonderful day.

Franklin sat at the back of the bus all the way home. He bumped up and down. He was so busy having fun that he almost forgot to get off at his stop.

His parents were waiting. "How is your tummy?" they asked.

Franklin looked puzzled. It had been such a good day that he had forgotten all about his jumpy tummy.

"My tummy is empty!" he said.

"That's a feeling that will go away, too," said Franklin's father.

"I made this for you," said Franklin's mother. She gave Franklin his favorite snack, fly pie.

"And I made this for you," said Franklin. He gave his parents two pictures and two big hugs.